Weekly Reader Children's
Book Club presents

THE
by James Holding, Jr.

WATCHCAT

Pictures by Marilyn Miller

Xerox Weekly Reader Family Books

XEROX

Publishing, Executive and Editorial Offices:
Xerox Weekly Reader Family Books
Middletown, Connecticut 06457

ISBN 0-88375-206-9
Library of Congress Catalogue Card Number: 74-17695

This book is for the three Janets in my
life—my wife, my granddaughter and my editor.

1
The Box

When they got off the yellow school bus on Friday afternoon, Jerry and Jessica Patterson never dreamed what a wonderful thing was waiting for them in the dirty cardboard box beside the path in the park.

The bus pulled up with a squeak of brakes. And Jerry, who was standing on the top step waiting for the door to be opened, turned and called out at the top of his voice, "Come on, Jess! This is our stop. How many times do I have to tell you?"

Jerry's twin sister, Jessica, standing only six inches behind him in the aisle of the bus, shot hot sparks of anger at him out of her brown eyes. As if she didn't know where to get off the bus without Jerry's telling her!

Wasn't she *older* than Jerry, born ten minutes before him, eight years ago last August? And wasn't she *bigger* than Jerry, four feet and half an inch to Jerry's four feet even? And wasn't she *smarter* than Jerry, too? At least in geography? So why did Jerry let on to all the other kids in the bus that she was too dumb to know where to get off?

Deep down, she knew the answer to that question. It was because Jerry thought it was fun to tease her. And the madder she got when he teased her, the more fun he thought it was. So Jessica usually pretended that Jerry's teasing didn't bother her a bit. That way, he stopped sooner. But there was never any real anger between Jerry and Jessica. They were twins, after all, which is just a little bit nicer than being plain brother and sister. And sometimes they were aware of a strong, deep current of understanding running between them that ordinary brothers and sisters seldom feel.

The bus door opened, and Jerry jumped to the ground with a whoop of triumph. Jessica followed him more sedately. Although she didn't whoop like her brother, she felt the same glow of happiness at putting another week of school behind them.

They were the only children to get off at Suburban Park. Without wasting a minute, they turned into the gravel path that led through the park to their house on Green Lane. Jessica was in the lead.

Halfway through the park, she stopped so suddenly that Jerry almost ran into her.

"What's the matter?" Jerry asked.

Jessica pointed. "Look!"

Under a forsythia bush beside the path was an old cardboard carton with a string around it. "Hey!" Jerry exclaimed in surprise. "Some litterburg threw that there, I bet."

"With a string tied around it?" asked Jessica.

They both looked at the box. After a moment, Jessica said in a tense whisper, "Jerry! It *moved*."

"I didn't see it move," Jerry said.

"Well, I did. It moved, all right."

The carton was about the size of one of the stereo speakers in their family room at home. Jerry murmured, "Why would it move, Jess?"

Jessica put on her high and mighty air. "Anybody would know that," she said. "There's something alive in it, that's why."

"Alive!" Jerry backed off a step from the box. A breeze rustled through the tops of the trees above their heads, making an eerie sound in the quiet park. "What do you think it is?"

Jessica shrugged her shoulders. "You're so smart about telling me when to get off the bus, you ought to be able to figure out a little thing like *that!*" She smiled at her brother, "Why don't you look inside, Jerry?"

Jerry's eyes had never left the box. "Hey! *I* saw it move, too!"

"I saw it first," said Jessica. Then, "Are you scared to look inside, Jerry?"

"You think I'm *afraid*?" cried Jerry, deeply wounded. "I'm not afraid of any old litterbug box!" He stood stock still in the path, all the same. Nothing about him moved except his Adam's apple, which bobbed up and down as he swallowed.

"Why don't you go see what's inside, then?" Jessica taunted.

"I'm going to, Jess," Jerry said. "I'm going to. Any minute now." When he got his nerve together, he took a deep breath and bent down to avoid the lower branches of the forsythia bush. Then he slowly and cautiously inched forward.

"Be careful!" Jessica warned him. Now that Jerry was taking positive action, her voice held a thread of worry.

Jerry aimed a half-hearted kick at the box when he was close enough. His shoe thudded against the side of the box.

And then a terrifying thing happened. Out of the closed carton rushed a wild, coughing wail of sound that made Jerry almost turn a somersault trying to get away from it. He slid back onto the path beside his sister, and out of sheer fright grabbed her hand, something he would never do if anybody was watching him.

Jessica turned pale. "Did you hear *that*!" she breathed, and held on to Jerry's hand very tightly.

For a second or two, the children stood there hand in hand, ready to run for their lives, waiting for that heart-freezing sound to be repeated. But whatever was in the box remained silent.

"Give it another kick," Jessica suggested at last.

"Kick it yourself," said Jerry. "It's your turn."

Jessica crept to the box. Greatly daring, she tapped on its side with her knuckles, the way you knock on a door.

Instantly, the same blood-curdling, coughing roar issued from the carton. This time it was Jessica who scrambled back to the path and seized Jerry's hand.

"Boy!" whispered Jerry. "It sounds like a tiger!"

"The box is too little for a tiger," Jessica pointed out.

"Not for a *little* tiger, it isn't," insisted Jerry.

Suddenly, as the strange roaring wail died away, the carton lid was lifted an inch or two by a strong upward surge of something inside. The lid jerked upward, time after time, and with each jerk upward, the lid pressed more strongly against the loosely-tied string around the carton.

Jerry pulled on Jessica's hand. "Run!" he yelled. "Come on, Jess! It's trying to get out!"

Jessica didn't budge. She said, "I *saw* something in there, Jerry. Under the lid. Something kind of brown and yellow. Like a big cat's head."

"It *is* a tiger!" Jerry cried. "Run, Jess!" He wasn't teasing now. He was very frightened and very anxious to save his sister from whatever mysterious danger lurked inside the box.

10

"It was a *regular* cat's head," said Jessica calmly. "I'm going to let the poor thing out of the box."

"You sure it's just a cat?" Jerry let go of his sister's hand.

"Stoop down. You can see its head when it pushes the lid up."

They squatted in the path and peered intently at the carton under the forsythia bush. Sure enough, the head of a cat showed for an instant in the opening the next time the lid rose.

Jerry felt much braver now. He said, "I'll let it out, Jess."
He pulled the box from its resting place under the bush into
the pathway. Then he gingerly worked the string off the end
of the carton.

As soon as the restraining string was gone, the box lid
popped wide open. And there, inside the carton, crouched the
most beautiful cat the children
had ever seen. It was a very
large cat, as cats go, but not as
big as a tiger, of course. It had

sleek, silky fur the color of coffee with rich cream in it. Its muzzle, paws, ear-tips, and the end of its tail were a glorious, deep, dark brown, like coffee *without* cream in it. Most surprising of all, this odd cat had blue eyes—as blue as the summer sky on a clear day.

Spellbound, Jerry and Jessica stared at the cat. and the cat stared crookedly back at them. Its china blue eyes were slightly crossed. Nobody made a sound.

Then, without any warning, the cat opened its dainty mouth and gave another nerve-shattering roar and leaped straight

out of its box onto Jessica's chest. It dug its claws gently into her sweater and hung on for dear life, looking up into her face and wailing very loudly.

Jessica jumped back in alarm. She uttered a shrill scream that was even louder than the cat's roar. Then, without thinking, she put up her hands to the silky creature clinging to her

chest. As though she'd turned a valve, the cat's hideous cater-
wauling ceased abruptly, and the strange creature snuggled
down contentedly into Jessica's arms, as tame and soft and
cuddly as a baby koala bear.

Jessica couldn't resist that. She began to stroke the cat's fur
and tickle its twitchy ears and croon small soothing sounds
to it. "It's darling!" she said finally, all fear gone. "Isn't it
sweet, Jerry?"

Jerry said, "Let me hold it."

Jessica passed the cat to him. She could tell Jerry liked it by the way he stroked the cat's back and put his cheek down against the satiny tan fur. So she said, "Let's take it home and keep it, Jerry."

Jerry said, "Yeah! Great!" Then he said doubtfully, "Do you think we'd be allowed?"

"Maybe," Jessica answered. "Mom likes cats."

"Dad doesn't, though," said Jerry, "and he's the boss."

"He might like this cat. And besides, he's no more boss than Mom is!"

"I bet they won't let us keep it, anyway," said Jerry gloomily.

"Let me hold her again," demanded Jessica, holding out her arms.

"It's a 'him', not a 'her'," said Jerry, passing the cat back to her.

"Why do you say that?"

Jerry laughed. "You ever know of a girl cat with a voice like a tiger?" He tried to imitate the cat's wailing coughing roar without success.

"Whether it's a boy or a girl, I want to keep it," said Jessica. "Don't you?"

"Sure."

"Let's take it home, then."

"Okay. You carry the cat. I'll carry the box."

"The box? What for?"

"To show Mom and Dad where we found the cat." Jerry

15

picked up the box. He glanced inside. "Hey!" he said. "There's a paper in here with writing on it. It's a note."

"What's it say?" Jessica asked.

Jerry read the note out loud. It wasn't very long. It said:

THIS IS A NICE CAT IF YOU CAN STAND THE NOISE. I CAN'T. SO YOU ARE WELCOME TO HIM.

That was all. No signature. No date. No address. Nothing else.

"See?" said Jerry. "What did I tell you? The note says 'him'. So it's a boy cat."

16

"So what?" said Jessica. "Come on." She started toward home, carrying the cat tenderly in her arms, while Jerry followed her, dragging the cardboard carton along by its flapping lid.

2

Family Conference

That evening, when Dad got home from the office, they had a conference in the family room. The family room was everybody's favorite. That's where the most comfortable chairs were, and Dad's books, and the color TV set, and the stereo, and Mom's sewing machine.

Mom spoke up first. She had on her white pants suit that Dad liked so much, and she was smiling, so Jerry and Jessica thought maybe she was on their side about the cat. She said to her husband, "The children found a cat today, Joe, and they want to keep it."

"Oh, no!" cried Dad and clasped his forehead. "Please! Not another stray cat, for Heaven's sake! I hope you told the twins we wouldn't stand for *that*!" He spoke as though Jessica and Jerry weren't even in the room with him.

"All I told them was, that as far as I'm concerned, they can keep the cat," Mom said, "*if* they promise, on their honor, to take complete care of it themselves."

Jerry and Jessica nodded eagerly. "We promised we would," Jessica piped up. "It's a darling cat, Daddy!"

"And you want me to make this very important decision?" Dad groaned. "All by myself? Do I have to decide *everything* in this family?"

Jessica said, "Yes, Daddy. Because Jerry says you're the boss."

Dad grinned at Mom and raised his bushy eyebrows. "But you know very well how I feel about stray cats!"

Mom said, "This isn't your plain, ordinary, regular, run-of-the-mill stray cat, Joe. This one is something special."

"They all are, to hear the twins tell it," said Dad. "What's so special about this one?"

"Well," said Mom, "for one thing, it's a Siamese cat."

"I know where Siam is, and Jerry doesn't," boasted Jessica. "Siam is called Thailand, now. I know that from geography."

Nobody paid any attention to that. Mom went on, "And furthermore, Joe, this is a quite a *large* cat the children found. A male cat." Mom paused. "And above all else, this is a cat with a very special kind of *voice*."

Dad grunted. "What's so special about his voice?"

"It's very loud," said Jessica.

"It sounds like a tiger!" said Jerry.

Dad winked at Mom. "Great!" he said. "That's all we need around this house. A cat with a voice like a tiger!"

Jerry said proudly, "It's really a terrific voice, Dad! Loud and scary. You'll see."

"I can hardly wait," Dad said. "Where *is* this loud voiced tiger of yours, anyway?"

"We tied him behind the garage until you came home," said

Jerry. "We didn't want him to scare you until you decided we could keep him."

Dad laughed. "Very thoughtful of you." He brooded for a minute in silence. Then he said, "I hope you haven't set your hearts on the cat, kids. Because I'm afraid you can't keep him."

"Why *not?*" asked Jessica and Jerry together.

"Because I suspect he's a valuable Siamese cat that belongs to somebody else. Somebody who is probably looking for him right now. Maybe they're even offering a big reward for him. So we can't keep him, can we? He isn't ours. We have to return him to his owner."

Jerry and Jessica didn't say anything. They waited for Mom to tell Dad about the note.

Slowly Mom took it out of her pocket and unfolded it, and held it out to Dad.

"What's this?" he asked.

Mom said, "It's a note from the cat's owner. It was in the

box with the cat when the children found it."

Dad read the note. Then he laughed. He thought Mom was playing a joke on him—that she had written the note herself. Mom said no, she certainly hadn't done any such thing. The note *was* in the box where they found the cat.

"The owner doesn't want his cat back, see?" Jerry said earnestly.

And Jessica wheedled, "Can we keep him, Daddy? Please, please?"

Dad looked at the faces of the twins. Then he looked at Mom. From the way she was smiling at him, he figured she was in favor of keeping the cat, too. He said, "Well, I guess I've been out-maneuvered and out-voted. Yes, kids, you can keep the cat."

Jessica and Jerry jumped up and down and yelled with excitement until Dad held up his hand for silence. "But only," he said solemnly, "if *I* can stand his noise! So trot your cat out here, kids, and let's hear him bellow, or whatever he does."

It was almost as if the cat knew he had to make a friend of Dad. For the minute Jerry and Jessica brought him proudly into the family room from behind the garage, he gave one of his long, loud, hair-raising roars and leaped right out of Jessica's arms onto Dad's shoulder, where he began to rub his head against Dad's ear.

Dad raised his hand to push the cat away. The cat rubbed against his hand, too. All Dad could think of to say was, "Loud and scary is right, Jerry! What a voice!"

Dad ended up stroking the cat.

3
The Watchcat

"What a voice!" Dad repeated.

"Yeah," said Jerry. "I told you. He could scare anybody, couldn't he, Dad?"

"He'll guard our house for us," Jessica put in happily. "He'll scare burglars away."

"And the Fuller Brush Man, and the Avon Lady, and the mailman, too!" Mom added with a laugh. Then she sobered, and said thoughtfully, "There *have* been some burglaries in the neighborhood recently, Joe."

"The cat will be our watchdog," Jessica said.

"Only he's really a watch*cat*!" Jerry said.

Everybody laughed at this funny idea. "I never heard of

a watchcat before," said Mom, "but our new cat certainly has the voice for it, I'll say that!"

Jessica kissed her father three times very quickly. Then she kissed the cat. "Thanks for letting us keep him, Daddy," she said. "What shall we call him?"

"Something like George," said Jerry. "That's a good name. How would George be?"

"That's awful!" Jessica protested. "If he was only a girl cat, we could call her Eleanore."

"Eleanore?" Mom looked at Jessica sharply. "Why Eleanore?"

Jessica giggled. "Because our cat's voice sounds something like Aunt Eleanore's."

"Now, Jessica!" Mom scolded her. Aunt Eleanore was Mom's sister. And she *did* have a loud voice.

"What do you think would be a good name, Mom?" Jessica asked.

Mom thought for a minute. "How about Ling-Ching? Something that sounds at least faintly Siamese," she suggested.

"I won't call my new cat by a dumb name like that!" Jerry objected. "Would you, Dad?" He appealed to his father.

Dad said, "You want to know what I'd call your watchcat?"

"What?" Mr. Patterson worked in an advertising agency and was used to thinking up good names for all sorts of things. Like soap and soft drinks and bug sprays.

"Well," Dad said slowly, "what about Tiger?"

"Great!" cried Jerry at once. "Tiger! On account of his voice. Sure!"

"Only we won't spell Tiger in the usual way," Dad went on. "We'll spell it T-H-A-I-G-E-R. Thai for Thailand. Get it? Only you *say* it just like Tiger."

"Oh!" said Jessica. "That's a wonderful idea, Daddy!"

Mom said Thaiger was all right with her if the children liked it, although she still thought Ling-Ching sounded kind of pretty.

"We'll have the name put on the cat's collar, so people will know how to spell it," Dad said.

Everybody said "Thaiger" over a few times to see how it sounded, and they all liked it. That settled the cat's name.

And at that moment the cat leaped from Dad's shoulder in one soaring bound to the top shelf of the bookcase. Standing up there beside a big sterling punchbowl that Mom and Dad got for a wedding present, he looked down at his new family. And he gave a great loud roar of happiness to show that he approved of his new name, too.

Mr. Patterson said, "If you ask me, that cat has either a bad case of whooping cough, or the epizootics. But never mind. We'll take him to the vet's right after dinner and have him checked. Okay?"

"Okay," everybody said.

4
Thaiger

So that's what they did.

And after the vet had examined their new watchcat, he told them two things: The first was that Thaiger didn't have whooping cough or epizootics or any other disease. Thaiger was a fine, healthy cat. The second thing he told them was that Thaiger had an oversized, badly deformed larynx, and that's what made his voice so loud and frightening.

"What's a larynx?" asked Jessica.

"His voice box," explained Dad.

"Oh," said Jerry. "We're lucky then. Because a good watch-cat *needs* a scary voice."

Thaiger soon became a part of the family. All the Patter-sons—even Dad—grew fond of him. For Thaiger not only had a scary, unusual voice to amuse them; he also did funny things that kept Jessica and Jerry constantly weak from laughter.

Take the finicky way Thaiger felt about fish, for instance. All cats are supposed to like fish for dinner once in a while. Not Thaiger. When Jessica or Jerry tried to give him some of their left-over fish from dinner, Thaiger would watch quietly while they dropped the bits of fish into his feeding bowl. Then slowly and politely, he would take the bits in his mouth, one by one, and stalk with great dignity to the wastebasket in the corner of the kitchen and drop them in. That's how he felt about ordinary fish—fish like bass, trout or fillet of sole. But it was a different story if the children put bits of *shellfish* in

his bowl—lobster Newburg, say, or sauteed shrimps, or soft-shell crab. Thaiger pounced on them at once with such enthusiasm and good appetite that he obviously found them delicious.

Or take the way Thaiger acted when he was thirsty. He wouldn't think of lapping water out of his dish on the floor. Not Thaiger. He preferred to bound up onto the kitchen sink and sit on its edge, roaring loudly to gain attention, until one of the twins turned on the cold water faucet and adjusted the flow to a tiny trickle about the thickness of a pencil. Then Thaiger would daintily place one soft paw in the bottom of the sink to support himself, and leaning far over, drink from the stream flowing out of the tap. Thaiger liked his drinking water to be *moving*. None of that still, insipid, stale water in a dish for him!

The funniest thing of all, the twins thought, was to watch Thaiger tangle with the record player in the family room. The first time Jerry and Jessica put on a record and started the turntable spinning, Thaiger approached curiously and watched the spinning record for a few moments. Then suddenly, with lightning speed, Thaiger leaped onto the turning record and scrabbled there, with his paws slipping and sliding, till he got his balance. Then he rode triumphantly around and around on the spinning disc as though he were on a merry-go-round especially made for him. Of course, after he scratched up that first record, the twins let him ride around on the record player without any record on it.

Jerry and Jessica tried to make an old quilt into a bed for Thaiger to sleep on, in the upstairs hall near their bedrooms. That didn't suit Thaiger at all. He selected his own sleeping place. And it wasn't in any upstairs hallway. It was in the silver punch bowl on the top shelf of Dad's bookcase in the

family room. If Thaiger was in the house at all, that's where he was usually to be found, either inside that silver bowl with his brown ears sticking over the edge of it, or lying cozily beside the bowl, looking down with sleepy blue eyes on the family room beneath him.

In fact, Thaiger seemed to like high places best. Outdoors, he climbed trees. He took naps on the top of Pattersons' car. And sometimes he went for a solitary ramble on the porch

roof, pretending to ignore any nearby birds, but really trying
very hard to sneak up on one and capture it for his dinner.

He never succeeded, thanks to the tiny bell on his collar
that Mr. Patterson had put there to warn the birds away.
Thaiger's name was on his collar, too, and the Pattersons' telephone number.

From his high perch on the top shelf of the bookcase in the
family room, Thaiger welcomed anyone who happened to en-
ter. Whether it was Jerry, Jessica, Mom, Dad or a perfect
stranger, Thaiger would greet them with a loud blood-curdling

roar and launch himself like a flying squirrel down onto the nearest shoulder or head.

The truth was, Thaiger loved people. All of them. Any of them. He loved Jerry and Jessica most, of course. But when he wanted to roar out his love and jump down into somebody's arms, *anybody* would do. Anybody at all.

This way of showing his love was unusual and unexpected. It was very frightening, too. Until Jessica and Jerry and Mom and Dad had warned all their friends about Thaiger's boisterous greeting, the big cat startled a lot of people into a state of deep shock.

But that's what a good watchcat is *supposed* to do, isn't it? Jerry and Jessica thought so. They firmly believed that Thaiger was just doing his job when he roared and jumped on people. They thought he was defending the treasures in the family room—the TV, the stereo, Dad's books, Mom's sewing machine—warning off intruders with his loud scary voice, attacking them like a bolt from heaven if they dared to set foot in the room.

Mr. and Mrs. Patterson didn't agree with the twins entirely. Mom and Dad claimed that Thaiger was nothing but a big bundle of love who could not, by any stretch of the imagination, even with his scary voice, ever be a really good watchcat. He liked people too much, they said.

It wasn't until one hot night in June, several months after the cat came to live with Jessica and Jerry, that the Pattersons found out who was right.

5

The Burglars

This is what happened.

After dinner, the Pattersons went off in their car to the movies in town. It was a picture about animals in Africa that they all wanted to see. Since they left before dark, they forgot to leave any lights on in the house. And that was a bad mistake.

At about ten o'clock, a truck drove slowly down Green Lane past Pattersons' house and stopped beside the curb two houses away. It was a van-type truck—like a little bus without any windows and two doors at the back for loading. It was painted gray all over.

There were two men in it—a tall, lanky, bald one and a shorter one with a straggly mustache drooping over the corners of his

mouth. Seeing the Pattersons' house so dark and deserted looking, they decided it might be a good house for them to rob that
night—if nobody was home, and if it had no burglar alarm sys-
tem to raise a fuss. And if there was no fierce watchdog around
to arouse the neighborhood.

The burglar with the mustache said to the bald one who was
driving the truck, "I'll go and have a look. You wait here." He
got out of the truck and walked back to Pattersons' house.

Five minutes later, he reappeared. "It's okay," he reported.
"Nobody home. No burglar alarms. And no watchdog. We can
drive right into the driveway and around back."

The truck drove around the block. This time, when it came
to Pattersons' house, it turned into their driveway just as
though it belonged there. The driver stopped the truck oppo-
site Pattersons' back door, out of sight from the street.

The burglars got out of the truck, leaving the motor running. They unlocked the back door with a skeleton key. Then, bold as brass, they walked into the Pattersons' kitchen as though they owned it. The tall burglar carried an empty burlap bag. The short one had a flashlight in his hand.

Once inside the house, they stood perfectly still for a time, straining their ears to be sure nobody was at home. The only noise they heard was the humming of the refrigerator.

"Okay," whispered the short burglar at last. Turning on his flashlight, he led the way into the dining room. There, Mrs. Patterson's monogrammed knives, forks and spoons of sterling silver were rapidly transferred from the buffet drawers to the robbers' burlap bag. They put her silver tea service into the bag, too. And her beautiful silver gravy-boat. And her two silver serving dishes.

Then the short burglar led the way with his flashlight down the hall toward Pattersons' family room. The tall burglar followed him, carrying the burlap bag, heavy now with all that silver in it.

6

The Blow

All this time, in his silver punchbowl on top the bookcase, Thaiger, the watchcat, had been sleeping peacefully. Peacefully, that is, except for a few jerks and twitches of his legs as he dreamed he was stalking a bird across the porch roof.

All at once, soft muffled footsteps in the hallway awakened him. He opened one eye and peered over the edge of his silver bed. He saw through the doorway a shaft of light piercing the darkness of the hall. Then two vague shapes appeared silently in the doorway of the family room. One shape was tall and thin. The other was shorter and fatter.

When the burglars came into the family room, Thaiger welcomed them in his usual way. Only he put a lot more energy into his greeting than he usually did, because he was a little lonesome without Jerry and Jessica and Mom and Dad, and he did love company, especially at night.

Thaiger's roar of welcome would have scared the stripes off a real tiger. It was a grunt, a cough, a scream, a wail, a yodel, a sob and a bellow, all mixed up together into one magnificently hideous shriek!

The burglars froze in their tracks. They stood as still as though somebody had nailed their feet to the floor. In pure terror, the short one raised his flashlight beam to see where that horrible roar was coming from—and also to see what kind of a weird monster could utter such a blood-curdling sound.

The flashlight beam, directed upward toward Thaiger's perch, showed the burglars a sight which did nothing to soothe their shattered nerves: A large cat, with creepy crossed eyes gleaming, and claw-armed paws wildly reaching, was hurtling down upon them like a deadly projectile from outer space. And it was aimed directly at the short burglar's head!

The droopy hair in his mustache stood straight up on end. Without thinking, without realizing what he was doing, he acted automatically to defend himself against Thaiger's attack from above.

He swung his heavy flashlight with all his might at the devil-cat descending upon him.

Poor Thaiger! He was trying so hard to be friendly and loving to his unexpected guests. And all he got in return was a dreadful blow on the head from the burglar's flashlight, and a sickening sense of falling, falling, falling into a huge pit of blackness.

The burglar pointed his flashlight beam at the floor. His hand was shaking very badly. "A cat!" he said in a choked voice. "Nothing but a crazy cat, Harry! I thought it was a tiger, at the very least! I thought we were dead!" He wiped the sweat off his forehead with his sleeve.

"Yeah!" Harry agreed. He was shaking too. He looked at Thaiger's still form on the carpet at their feet. "I guess you fixed him, though, Bud. Whew!"

"Get that silver bowl up there on the bookcase," Bud said. "Then help me with this."

Harry added Thaiger's silver punchbowl to the contents of burlap bag.

Bud unplugged the TV set. Harry dropped his burlap bag on the floor and picked up one end of the TV set while Bud lifted the other. "Okay," Bud said, and they carefully carried the TV set between them out through the kitchen to their waiting truck.

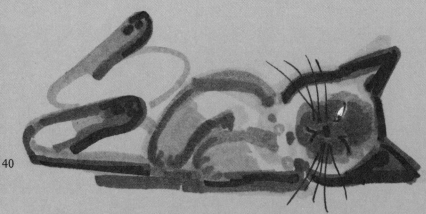

40

7

The Bowl

While they were gone, Thaiger stirred. He opened one blue eye. He saw nothing but darkness. He was hurt, bewildered, alone. He tried to stand up. He was too weak; his legs buckled under his weight. He sniffed mournfully, trying to understand what was happening to him.

That forlorn sniff brought him a whiff of a familiar odor— the clean, metallic smell of his silver bed. It made poor Thaiger yearn with all his heart to curl up in that familiar bed and forget all about this awful nightmare he was having.

He dragged himself a few inches across the rug toward the punchbowl smell. He bumped into something lumpy and rough. What was that? He was terribly confused, only half conscious. But he was sure of one thing. He was sure he smelled his own silver bed inside that bag! The comfortable, shiny bed he longed for. Slowly, an inch at a time, he clawed his dazed way into the bag himself.

Sure enough, there, inside, was his bed! Thaiger collapsed into it thankfully. Before he could get really comfortable, though, he fell into that bottomless pit of black unconsciousness again.

The burglars came back into the family room and carried the stereo speakers out to their truck. Then they took Thaiger's merry-go-round, the record-player. Last of all, Harry closed up the mouth of his burlap sack full of silverware, carried it outside and tossed it into the back of the truck with the TV set and the stereo.

Then the truck drove away.

8

The Detective

At eleven o'clock the next morning, the Pattersons had another conference in their family room. This time, though, there was a fifth person present: Detective Donald Peters.

The detective said, "And you didn't discover that you'd been robbed until this morning, Mrs. Patterson?"

Mom said, "No. We didn't get home from the movies until quite late. We all went straight to bed without looking in this room at all."

"And you found your back door unlocked this morning?" the detective asked Dad. He was writing down everything in a black notebook on his knee.

"Yes," Dad answered. "And I'm sure it was locked when we left for the movies."

The detective nodded, and wrote down: *Thieves entered by rear door*. Then he said to Mom, "May I have a list of the missing items, please?"

As Mom told him each thing, he wrote it down in his notebook: *color TV set, stereo, monogrammed flat silver (JPM), silver gravy boat, serving dishes, punchbowl* . . .

When Mom got that far, Jerry couldn't hold back any longer. He was practically dancing with impatience. "We don't care about any of *that* stuff!" he burst out. "We want *Thaiger* back! He's the most important thing!"

Detective Peters said, "Thaiger?"

Jessica spoke up in a trembly voice. She was close to tears, thinking about poor Thaiger in the hands of cruel burglars. " Thaiger's our watchcat," she explained.

Detective Peters looked at Dad. "What's this watchcat business?" You mean a cat is missing, too? Or does your daughter mean a watch*dog*?"

"A watch*cat*!" Jerry said, before Dad could say anything. "He's a Siamese cat. And he sleeps in that bowl that you've written down that the robbers stole from up there." Jerry pointed at the top bookshelf. "And I bet the robbers took Thaiger when they stole his bed!"

This explanation seemed to confuse the detective slightly. But before he could ask any more questions, the telephone rang. It was on the round table beside Dad's chair. He picked up the receiver and said, "Hello."

Then they heard him say, "Yes, this is 913-6843. Pattersons' residence." The person at the other end of the line said something. Dad's bushy eyebrows rose clear up into his hair in surprise. "What? What's that?" he asked. Suddenly he sounded very excited. "Yes!" he cried then. "Yes! We *do* own a cat named Thaiger!"

Dad put his hand over the mouthpiece and said, "Jessica, Jerry! Somebody's found Thaiger!"

Jerry yelled, "Oh, boy!" at the top of his voice.

Jessica started to cry.

They both ran over to their father's chair and tried to hear the rest of the telephone conversation. Dad held the receiver away from his ear a little. A man's voice was saying over the wire, " . . . found your telephone number on the cat's collar.

And I found the *cat* in a kind of a funny place. Want to come and get him?"

"Yes!" shouted Jerry and Jessica, forgetting that they weren't the ones being asked.

Dad said, "Sure, Mr. Carter, sure. Fine! We'll be there in no time! What's your address?" Dad wrote it down.

When he hung up the phone, everybody started talking at once. Detective Peters closed his notebook with a snap. He raised his hand and said, "Quiet, please!" in a loud voice. Everyone shut up right away. The detective went on, "If somebody has found your—ah—watchcat, that's a clue! So when you go to pick up your cat, I'm going along." Then he looked at the rapt expression on the twins' faces and said, "On second thought, maybe *you'd* better ride with me in *my* car."

Jerry breathed "Oh, boy!" again.

Jessica stopped crying.

Jerry said, "Can we use the siren?"

And the detective grinned and said, "Sure, why not? Let's go!"

9
The Garage

Jessica and Jerry said afterward that that was probably the nicest auto ride they had ever had in their whole lives. First, because they were going to get their watchcat back, safe and sound, at the end of the ride. Second, because they were riding in a real police car with a siren. Other cars got out of their way like magic.

Mr. Carter, the man who had found Thaiger, lived way over on the north side of the city. When Detective Peters and the Pattersons got to his house, he was walking up and down the sidewalk in front of it, waiting for them. He carried something brown and tan in his arms.

"There's Thaiger!" shouted Jerry, jumping out of the police

car. "Hey, Thaiger! Are you okay? Hello, Thaiger!"

The minute Thaiger heard Jerry's voice, he jumped straight out of Mr. Carter's arms onto Jerry's shoulder and howled a tremendous roar right into Jerry's ear. Then Thaiger jumped

from Jerry's shoulder to Jessica's arms, and gave *her* a big wail of welcome. Mom and Dad couldn't help laughing when they saw how glad Thaiger was to see the twins again.

As for Detective Peters, he just stood for a second with his mouth hanging open in amazement. He had never heard a cat make a noise like that before. At last he said to Mr. Carter, who was a thin, white-haired man with thick eyeglasses, "I'm Detective Peters from the Police Department. You said you found this cat in a funny place. Where?"

Mr. Carter pointed. "Next door there," he said. "In the garage."

"In the garage?" Jessica said.

"Tell me about it," the detective said.

They all sat down in chairs on Mr. Carter's front porch, all except Thaiger. He sat in Jessica's lap.

"I woke up earlier than usual this morning," Mr. Carter began, "and I heard this terrible roaring noise coming through
my open window."

"That was old Thaiger, I bet!" cried Jerry. "He's got a great
voice, Mr. Carter!"

"He surely has! Well, I tried to go back to sleep again, but I couldn't. I kept hearing that awful racket. The more I listened to it, the more it seemed to me as though some poor animal or other—I didn't know it was a *cat* then—was suffering terrible tortures and needed help." Mr. Carter looked around at his guests and said politely, "Anybody like any iced tea? It's fine on a hot day like this."

"No, thank you!" everybody said quickly. They wanted Mr. Carter to go on with his story.

Jessica said breathlessly, "Then what happened, Mr. Carter?"

"Well, I got dressed and went outside. I listened and listened to that noise. And I finally figured out it was coming from the garage at the back of the house next door. You've got to understand that house next door has been empty for years. Falling down from old age, matter of fact. And the garage is no better. So I thought it was mighty funny, some animal having a fit or something in the garage of a house where nobody lives. Wouldn't you?"

Everybody hurriedly said they would.

"So I peeked through a crack in the garage door," Mr. Carter said, closing one eye to illustrate, "and what do you think I saw in there?"

"Thaiger!" guessed Jerry and Jessica together.

Mr. Carter wagged his head and grinned. "Nope. I saw a gray truck, that's what. Just sitting there! Remember now, in a garage of a house where nobody has lived for years. A new truck! And that awful noise was coming from the back of that truck!"

52

Thaiger gave a strangled roar, as though agreeing with Mr. Carter.

"The old garage door had a brand new padlock on it. So I went around the side of the garage and climbed in a window.

Then I opened the doors of the truck, and that fellow there—"
Mr. Carter nodded at Thaiger—"jumped right onto my chest
with the most hair-raising scream I ever heard! Thought for
a minute I was going to have a heart attack!"

Jessica leaned down and kissed Thaiger between the ears.
"He's pretty scary, isn't he?" she asked proudly.

"Well, I calmed the cat down and looked on his collar," Mr. Carter finished, "and there was your telephone number."

"Gee, Mr. Carter, you're the greatest!" Jerry said.

"You're better than that!" said Jessica. "Thank you!" She hugged Thaiger.

Detective Peters said, "Will you show me this truck where you found Thaiger?"

"Sure," agreed Mr. Carter. "Come on."

While the detective went next door with Mr. Carter, the Pattersons and Thaiger stayed on Mr. Carter's porch. Pretty soon, the detective and Mr. Carter came back. Detective Peters was smiling. "There's a TV set, a stereo, and a burlap bag full of silverware in that truck next door," he said. "The monogram on the silver is JPM."

Mom gave a big sigh of relief. "That's ours. May we have our things back?"

"In a day or two," said the detective. "That is, if you are willing to let me keep them temporarily."

"What for?" Dad asked.

"Whoever stole them from you owns that truck next door. And the thieves will come back for that truck and what's in it. They probably use the vacant garage to hide their truck in until they can transfer the things to a safer place. You see? I'm sure they'll be back to pick up their truck. And when they do . . . we'll be waiting for them."

"Ooh!" said Jessica. "A trap! What a super idea!"

"Okay," said Dad. "Keep the stuff as long as you need it. Can we take Thaiger home now?"

"Sure," said Detective Peters. He looked at Thaiger, sitting in Jessica's lap, with a new respect. "That's some watchcat, all right," he said admiringly. "Got right into the truck with your stolen things and stuck with them until the burglars left. Then he yelled for help and brought Mr. Carter to the rescue. He's a real watchcat. I'm sorry I thought at first you meant a watchdog, Jessica."

"That's okay," said Jessica generously. "There aren't too many watchcats around, I guess."

Detective Peters called on his car radio for another police car to come to Mr. Carter's house and take the Pattersons home again. He was going to stay at Mr. Carter's and wait for the burglars to return for their truck.

The last thing Dad said to him was, "Let us know how your trap works out, will you?"

"I'll be in touch with you," promised Detective Peters.

10
The Hero

Two days later, Detective Peters showed up at the Pattersons' house just before dinnertime. The twins were home from school and Dad was home from the office. "Glad you're all here," said the detective. "I can make my report to everybody at once."

"Did you catch the burglars?" asked Jessica.

"Are we going to get Thaiger's merry-go-round back?" asked Jerry.

"The answer to both questions is 'yes'," said Peters, smiling at the children. "We caught the burglars all right. But first, we let them lead us in their truck to an old warehouse in Waterdale where they stored the stuff they stole until they could sell it. Dozens of TV sets and stereos and tons of silverware! That seems to be what they specialized in. And every single item stolen from some home in this city by the same robbers who robbed you!"

Jerry said, "Wow!" very loud.

"I don't mind telling you," the detective went on, "that because of your watchcat's work, we've been able to close the books on twenty-seven unsolved burglaries. And get most of the stolen goods back. Twenty-seven!" Detective Peters smiled. "In fact, as a result of this case, I've been promoted to detective, second class, myself!"

"Congratulations!" said Dad. He shook hands with Detective Peters.

"Thanks," said the detective. "Before I leave you, there's one more thing." He reached into his pocket and brought out a tiny silver tag on a short silver chain. "I told all the fellows down at the Police Department about your watchcat and how he helped me to catch the burglars. And we all decided we should do something to show Thaiger our appreciation." Detective Peters bounced the little tag up and down on the palm of his hand. "So we had this little medal made for him."

"For Thaiger?" cried Jerry happily. He looked up at the top shelf of the bookcase, where Thaiger was sitting, "You hear that, Thaiger?"

Detective Peters handed the silver tag to Jessica. "We'd like Thaiger to wear this on his collar, with his name and his bell and your telephone number. Kind of like a policeman's shield, understand?"

"What's it say?" asked Mom, craning to see the silver tag.

"Read it to us, Jess," said Dad.

Jessica went over to the window where there was enough

light for her to read the tiny letters on the medal. She read them out loud:

WATCHCAT DETECTIVE

FIRST CLASS

Thaiger looked down sleepily from his perch on the bookcase. He heard Jessica say his name and read something from the shiny thing in her hand. Then he heard all the others laughing and clapping and shouting, "Hurray for Thaiger!" and "Three cheers for our watchcat!" He didn't know what was going on, but he had a feeling they were all saying something very nice indeed about *him*.

So he drew in a deep breath and roared the loudest roar he could manage and launched himself straight down onto Detective Peters' head.